Studies of I

(from Literary Friends and Acquaintance)

William Dean Howells

Alpha Editions

This edition published in 2024

ISBN : 9789364737647

Design and Setting By
Alpha Editions
www.alphaedis.com
Email - info@alphaedis.com

As per information held with us this book is in Public Domain.
This book is a reproduction of an important historical work. Alpha Editions uses the best technology to reproduce historical work in the same manner it was first published to preserve its original nature. Any marks or number seen are left intentionally to preserve its true form.

STUDIES OF LOWELL

I have already spoken of my earliest meetings with Lowell at Cambridge when I came to New England on a literary pilgrimage from the West in 1860. I saw him more and more after I went to live in Cambridge in 1866; and I now wish to record what I knew of him during the years that passed between this date and that of his death. If the portrait I shall try to paint does not seem a faithful likeness to others who knew him, I shall only claim that so he looked to me, at this moment and at that. If I do not keep myself quite out of the picture, what painter ever did?

I.

It was in the summer of 1865 that I came home from my consular post at Venice; and two weeks after I landed in Boston, I went out to see Lowell at Elmwood, and give him an inkstand that I had brought him from Italy. The bronze lobster whose back opened and disclosed an inkpot and a sand-box was quite ugly; but I thought it beautiful then, and if Lowell thought otherwise he never did anything to let me know it. He put the thing in the middle of his writing-table (he nearly always wrote on a pasteboard pad resting upon his knees), and there it remained as long as I knew the place— a matter of twenty-five years; but in all that time I suppose the inkpot continued as dry as the sand-box.

My visit was in the heat of August, which is as fervid in Cambridge as it can well be anywhere, and I still have a sense of his study windows lifted to the summer night, and the crickets and grasshoppers crying in at them from the lawns and the gardens outside. Other people went away from Cambridge in the summer to the sea and to the mountains, but Lowell always stayed at Elmwood, in an impassioned love for his home and for his town. I must have found him there in the afternoon, and he must have made me sup with him (dinner was at two o'clock) and then go with him for a long night of talk in his study. He liked to have some one help him idle the time away, and keep him as long as possible from his work; and no doubt I was impersonally serving his turn in this way, aside from any pleasure he might have had in my company as some one he had always been kind to, and as a fresh arrival from the Italy dear to us both.

He lighted his pipe, and from the depths of his easychair, invited my shy youth to all the ease it was capable of in his presence. It was not much; I loved him, and he gave me reason to think that he was fond of me, but in Lowell I was always conscious of an older and closer and stricter civilization than my own, an unbroken tradition, a more authoritative status. His democracy was more of the head and mine more of the heart, and his denied the equality which mine affirmed. But his nature was so noble and his reason so tolerant that whenever in our long acquaintance I found it well to come to open rebellion, as I more than once did, he admitted my right of insurrection, and never resented the outbreak. I disliked to differ with him, and perhaps he subtly felt this so much that he would not dislike me for doing it. He even suffered being taxed with inconsistency, and where he saw that he had not been quite just, he would take punishment for his error, with a contrition that was sometimes humorous and always touching.

Just then it was the dark hour before the dawn with Italy, and he was interested but not much encouraged by what I could tell him of the feeling in Venice against the Austrians. He seemed to reserve a like scepticism concerning the fine things I was hoping for the Italians in literature, and he confessed an interest in the facts treated which in the retrospect, I am aware, was more tolerant than participant of my enthusiasm. That was always Lowell's attitude towards the opinions of people he liked, when he could not go their lengths with them, and nothing was more characteristic of his affectionate nature and his just intelligence. He was a man of the most strenuous convictions, but he loved many sorts of people whose convictions he disagreed with, and he suffered even prejudices counter to his own if they were not ignoble. In the whimsicalities of others he delighted as much as in his own.

II.

Our associations with Italy held over until the next day, when after breakfast he went with me towards Boston as far as "the village": for so he liked to speak of Cambridge in the custom of his younger days when wide tracts of meadow separated Harvard Square from his life-long home at Elmwood. We stood on the platform of the horsecar together, and when I objected to his paying my fare in the American fashion, he allowed that the Italian usage of each paying for himself was the politer way. He would not commit himself about my returning to Venice (for I had not given up my place, yet, and was away on leave), but he intimated his distrust of the flattering conditions of life abroad. He said it was charming to be treated 'da signore', but he seemed to doubt whether it was well; and in this as in all other things he showed his final fealty to the American ideal.

It was that serious and great moment after the successful close of the civil war when the republican consciousness was more robust in us than ever before or since; but I cannot recall any reference to the historical interest of the time in Lowell's talk. It had been all about literature and about travel;

and now with the suggestion of the word village it began to be a little about his youth. I have said before how reluctant he was to let his youth go from him; and perhaps the touch with my juniority had made him realize how near he was to fifty, and set him thinking of the past which had sorrows in it to age him beyond his years. He would never speak of these, though he often spoke of the past. He told once of having been on a brief journey when he was six years old, with his father, and of driving up to the gate of Elmwood in the evening, and his father saying, "Ah, this is a pleasant place! I wonder who lives here—what little boy?" At another time he pointed out a certain window in his study, and said he could see himself standing by it when he could only get his chin on the window-sill. His memories of the house, and of everything belonging to it, were very tender; but he could laugh over an escapade of his youth when he helped his fellow-students pull down his father's fences, in the pure zeal of good-comradeship.

III.

My fortunes took me to New York, and I spent most of the winter of 1865-6 writing in the office of 'The Nation'. I contributed several sketches of Italian travel to that paper; and one of these brought me a precious letter from Lowell. He praised my sketch, which he said he had read without the least notion who had written it, and he wanted me to feel the full value of such an impersonal pleasure in it. At the same time he did not fail to tell me that he disliked some pseudo-cynical verses of mine which he had read in another place; and I believe it was then that he bade me "sweat the Heine out of" me, "as men sweat the mercury out of their bones."

When I was asked to be assistant editor of the Atlantic Monthly, and came on to Boston to talk the matter over with the publishers, I went out to Cambridge and consulted Lowell. He strongly urged me to take the position (I thought myself hopefully placed in New York on The Nation); and at the same time he seemed to have it on his heart to say that he had recommended some one else for it, never, he owned, having thought of me.

He was most cordial, but after I came to live in Cambridge (where the magazine was printed, and I could more conveniently look over the proofs), he did not call on me for more than a month, and seemed quite to have forgotten me. We met one night at Mr. Norton's, for one of the Dante readings, and he took no special notice of me till I happened to say something that offered him a chance to give me a little humorous snub. I was speaking of a paper in the Magazine on the "Claudian Emissary," and I demanded (no doubt a little too airily) something like "Who in the world ever heard of the Claudian Emissary?" "You are in Cambridge, Mr. Howells," Lowell answered, and laughed at my confusion. Having put me down, he seemed to soften towards me, and at parting he said, with a light of half-mocking tenderness in his beautiful eyes, "Goodnight, fellow-townsman." "I hardly knew we were fellow-townsmen," I returned. He liked that, apparently, and said he had been meaning to call upon me; and that he was coming very soon.

He was as good as his word, and after that hardly a week of any kind of weather passed but he mounted the steps to the door of the ugly little house in which I lived, two miles away from him, and asked me to walk. These walks continued, I suppose, until Lowell went abroad for a winter in the early seventies. They took us all over Cambridge, which he knew and loved every inch of, and led us afield through the straggling, unhandsome outskirts, bedrabbled with squalid Irish neighborhoods, and fraying off into marshes and salt meadows. He liked to indulge an excess of admiration for the local landscape, and though I never heard him profess a preference for the Charles River flats to the finest Alpine scenery, I could well believe he would do so under provocation of a fit listener's surprise. He had always so much of the boy in him that he liked to tease the over-serious or over-sincere. He liked to tease and he liked to mock, especially his juniors, if any touch of affectation, or any little exuberance of manner gave him the chance; when he once came to fetch me, and the young mistress of the house entered with a certain excessive elasticity, he sprang from his seat, and minced towards her, with a burlesque of her buoyant carriage which made her laugh. When he had given us his heart in trust of ours, he used us like a younger brother and sister; or like his own children. He included our children in his affection, and he enjoyed our fondness for them as if it were something that had come back to him from his own youth. I think he had also a sort of artistic, a sort of ethical pleasure in it, as being of the good tradition, of the old honest, simple material, from which pleasing effects in literature and civilization were wrought. He liked giving the children books, and writing tricksy fancies in these, where he masked as a fairy prince; and as long as he lived he remembered his early kindness for them.

IV.

In those walks of ours I believe he did most of the talking, and from his talk then and at other times there remains to me an impression of his growing conservatism. I had in fact come into his life when it had spent its impulse towards positive reform, and I was to be witness of its increasing tendency towards the negative sort. He was quite past the storm and stress of his anti-slavery age; with the close of the war which had broken for him all his ideals of inviolable peace, he had reached the age of misgiving. I do not mean that I ever heard him express doubt of what he had helped to do, or regret for what he had done; but I know that he viewed with critical anxiety what other men were doing with the accomplished facts. His anxiety gave a cast of what one may call reluctance from the political situation, and turned him back towards those civic and social defences which he had once seemed willing to abandon. I do not mean that he lost faith in democracy; this faith he constantly then and signally afterwards affirmed; but he certainly had no longer any faith in insubordination as a means of grace. He preached a quite Socratic reverence for law, as law, and I remember that once when I had got back from Canada in the usual disgust for the American custom-house, and spoke lightly of smuggling as not an evil in itself, and perhaps even a right under our vexatious tariff, he would not have it, but held that the illegality of the act made it a moral offence. This was not the logic that would have justified the attitude of the anti-slavery men towards the fugitive slave act; but it was in accord with Lowell's feeling about John Brown, whom he honored while always condemning his violation of law; and it was in the line of all his later thinking. In this, he wished you to agree with him, or at least he wished to make you; but he did not wish you to be more of his mind than he was himself. In one of those squalid Irish neighborhoods I confessed a grudge (a mean and cruel grudge, I now think it) for the increasing presence of that race among us, but this did not please him; and I am sure that whatever misgiving he had as to the future of America, he would not have had it less than it had been the refuge and opportunity of the poor of any race or color. Yet he would not have had it this alone. There was a line in his poem on Agassiz which he left out of the printed version, at the fervent entreaty of his friends, as saying too bitterly his disappointment with his country. Writing at the distance of Europe, and with America in the perspective which the alien environment clouded, he spoke of her as "The Land of Broken Promise." It was a splendid reproach, but perhaps too dramatic to bear the full test of analysis, and yet it had the truth in it, and might, I think, have usefully stood, to the end of making people think. Undoubtedly it expressed his sense of the case, and in the same measure it would now express that of many who love their country most among us. It is well to hold one's country to her promises, and if there are any who think she is forgetting them it is their duty to say so, even to the point of bitter accusation. I do not suppose it was the "common man" of Lincoln's dream that Lowell thought America was unfaithful to, though as I have suggested he could be tender of the common man's hopes in her; but he was impeaching in that blotted line her sincerity with the uncommon man: the man who had expected of her a constancy to the ideals of her youth end to the high martyr-moods of the war which had given an unguarded and bewildering freedom to a race of slaves. He was thinking of the shame of our municipal corruptions, the debased quality of our national statesmanship, the decadence of our whole civic tone, rather than of the increasing disabilities of the hard-working poor, though his heart when he thought of them was with them, too, as it was in "the time when the slave would not let him sleep."

He spoke very rarely of those times, perhaps because their political and social associations were so knit up with the saddest and tenderest personal memories, which it was still anguish to touch. Not only was he

"—not of the race That hawk, their
sorrows in the market place,"

but so far as my witness went he shrank from mention of them. I do not remember hearing him speak of the young wife who influenced him so potently at the most vital moment, and turned him from his whole scholarly and aristocratic tradition to an impassioned championship of the oppressed; and he never spoke of the children he had lost. I recall but one allusion to the days when he was fighting the anti-slavery battle along the whole line, and this was with a humorous relish of his Irish servant's disgust in having to wait upon a negro whom he had asked to his table.

He was rather severe in his notions of the subordination his domestics owed him. They were "to do as they were bid," and yet he had a tenderness for such as had been any time with him, which was wounded when once a hired man long in his employ greedily overreached him in a certain transaction. He complained of that with a simple grief for the man's indelicacy after so many favors from him, rather than with any resentment. His hauteur towards his dependents was theoretic; his actual behavior was of the gentle consideration common among Americans of good breeding, and that recreant hired man had no doubt never been suffered to exceed him in shows of mutual politeness. Often when the maid was about weightier matters, he came and opened his door to me himself, welcoming me with the smile that was like no other. Sometimes he said, "Siete il benvenuto," or used some other Italian phrase, which put me at ease with him in the region where we were most at home together.

Looking back I must confess that I do not see what it was he found to make him wish for my company, which he presently insisted upon having once a week at dinner. After the meal we turned into his study where we sat before a wood fire in winter, and he smoked and talked. He smoked a pipe which was always needing tobacco, or going out, so that I have the figure of him before my eyes constantly getting out of his deep chair to rekindle it from the fire with a paper lighter. He was often out of his chair to get a book from the shelves that lined the walls, either for a passage which he wished to read, or for some disputed point which he wished to settle. If I had caused the dispute, he enjoyed putting me in the wrong; if he could not, he sometimes whimsically persisted in his error, in defiance of all authority; but mostly he had such reverence for the truth that he would not question it even in jest.

If I dropped in upon him in the afternoon I was apt to find him reading the old French poets, or the plays of Calderon, or the 'Divina Commedia', which he magnanimously supposed me much better acquainted with than I was because I knew some passages of it by heart. One day I came in quoting

> "Io son, cantava, io son dolce Sirena,
> Che i marinai in mezzo al mar dismago."

He stared at me in a rapture with the matchless music, and then uttered all his adoration and despair in one word. "Damn!" he said, and no more. I believe he instantly proposed a walk that day, as if his study walls with all their vistas into the great literatures cramped his soul liberated to a sense of ineffable beauty of the verse of the 'somma poeta'. But commonly be preferred to have me sit down with him there among the mute witnesses of the larger part of his life. As I have suggested in my own case, it did not matter much whether you brought anything to the feast or not. If he liked you he liked being with you, not for what he got, but for what he gave. He was fond of one man whom I recall as the most silent man I ever met. I never heard him say anything, not even a dull thing, but Lowell delighted in him, and would have you believe that he was full of quaint humor.

V.

While Lowell lived there was a superstition, which has perhaps survived him, that he was an indolent man, wasting himself in barren studies and minor efforts instead of devoting his great powers to some monumental work worthy of them. If the robust body of literature, both poetry and prose, which lives after him does not yet correct this vain delusion, the time will come when it must; and in the meantime the delusion cannot vex him now. I think it did vex him, then, and that he even shared it, and tried at times to meet such shadowy claim as it had. One of the things that people urged upon him was to write some sort of story, and it is known how he attempted this in verse. It is less known that he attempted it in prose, and that he went so far as to write the first chapter of a novel. He read this to me, and though I praised it then, I have a feeling now that if he had finished the novel it would have been a failure. "But I shall never finish it," he sighed, as if he felt irremediable defects in it, and laid the manuscript away, to turn and light his pipe. It was a rather old-fashioned study of a whimsical character, and it did not arrive anywhere, so far as it went; but I believe that it might have been different with a Yankee story in verse such as we have fragmentarily in 'The Nooning' and 'FitzAdam's Story'. Still, his gift was essentially lyrical and meditative, with the universal New England tendency to allegory. He was wholly undramatic in the actuation of the characters which he imagined so dramatically. He liked to deal with his subject at first hand, to indulge through himself all the whim and fancy which the more dramatic talent indulges through its personages.

He enjoyed writing such a poem as "The Cathedral," which is not of his best, but which is more immediately himself, in all his moods, than some better poems. He read it to me soon after it was written, and in the long walk which we went hard upon the reading (our way led us through the Port far towards East Cambridge, where he wished to show me a tupelo-tree of his acquaintance, because I said I had never seen one), his talk was still of the poem which he was greatly in conceit of. Later his satisfaction with it received a check from the reserves of other friends concerning some whimsical lines which seemed to them too great a drop from the higher moods of the piece. Their reluctance nettled him; perhaps he agreed with them; but he would not change the lines, and they stand as he first wrote them. In fact, most of his lines stand as he first wrote them; he would often change them in revision, and then, in a second revision go back to the first version.

He was very sensitive to criticism, especially from those he valued through his head or heart. He would try to hide his hurt, and he would not let you speak of it, as though your sympathy unmanned him, but you could see that he suffered. This notably happened in my remembrance from a review in a journal which he greatly esteemed; and once when in a notice of my own I had put one little thorny point among the flowers, he confessed a puncture from it. He praised the criticism hardily, but I knew that he winced under my recognition of the didactic quality which he had not quite guarded himself against in the poetry otherwise praised. He liked your liking, and he openly rejoiced in it; and I suppose he made himself believe that in trying his verse with his friends he was testing it; but I do not believe that he was, and I do not think he ever corrected his judgment by theirs, however he suffered from it.

In any matter that concerned literary morals he was more than eager to profit by another eye. One summer he sent me for the Magazine a poem which, when I read it, I trembled to find in motive almost exactly like one we had lately printed by another contributor. There was nothing for it but to call his attention to the resemblance, and I went over to Elmwood with the two poems. He was not at home, and I was obliged to leave the poems, I suppose with some sort of note, for the next morning's post brought me a delicious letter from him, all one cry of confession, the most complete, the most ample. He did not trouble himself to say that his poem was an unconscious reproduction of the other; that was for every reason unnecessary, but he had at once rewritten it upon wholly different lines; and I do not think any reader was reminded of Mrs. Akers's "Among the Laurels" by Lowell's "Foot-path." He was not only much more sensitive of others' rights than his own, but in spite of a certain severity in him, he was most tenderly regardful of their sensibilities when he had imagined them: he did not always imagine them.

VI.

At this period, between the years 1866 and 1874, when he unwillingly went abroad for a twelvemonth, Lowell was seen in very few Cambridge houses, and in still fewer Boston houses. He was not an unsocial man, but he was most distinctly not a society man. He loved chiefly the companionship of books, and of men who loved books; but of women generally he had an amusing diffidence; he revered them and honored them, but he would rather not have had them about. This is over-saying it, of course, but the truth is in what I say. There was never a more devoted husband, and he was content to let his devotion to the sex end with that. He especially could not abide difference of opinion in women; he valued their taste, their wit, their humor, but he would have none of their reason. I was by one day when he was arguing a point with one of his nieces, and after it had gone on for some time, and the impartial witness must have owned that she was getting the better of him he closed the controversy by giving her a great kiss, with the words, "You are a very good girl, my dear," and practically putting her out of the room. As to women of the flirtatious type, he did not dislike them; no man, perhaps, does; but he feared them, and he said that with them there was but one way, and that was to run.

I have a notion that at this period Lowell was more freely and fully himself than at any other. The passions and impulses of his younger manhood had mellowed, the sorrows of that time had softened; he could blamelessly live to himself in his affections and his sobered ideals. His was always a duteous life; but he had pretty well given up making man over in his own image, as we all wish some time to do, and then no longer wish it. He fulfilled his obligations to his fellow-men as these sought him out, but he had ceased to seek them. He loved his friends and their love, but he had apparently no desire to enlarge their circle. It was that hour of civic suspense, in which public men seemed still actuated by unselfish aims, and one not essentially a politician might contentedly wait to see what would come of their doing their best. At any rate, without occasionally withholding open criticism or acclaim Lowell waited among his books for the wounds of the war to heal themselves, and the nation to begin her healthfuller and nobler life. With slavery gone, what might not one expect of American democracy!

His life at Elmwood was of an entire simplicity. In the old colonial mansion in which he was born, he dwelt in the embowering leafage, amid the quiet of lawns and garden-plots broken by few noises ruder than those from the elms and the syringas where

"The oriole clattered and the cat-bird sang."

From the tracks on Brattle Street, came the drowsy tinkle of horse-car bells; and sometimes a funeral trailed its black length past the corner of his grounds, and lost itself from sight under the shadows of the willows that hid Mount Auburn from his study windows. In the winter the deep New England snows kept their purity in the stretch of meadow behind the house, which a double row of pines guarded in a domestic privacy. All was of a modest dignity within and without the house, which Lowell loved but did not imagine of a manorial presence; and he could not conceal his annoyance with an over-enthusiastic account of his home in which the simple chiselling of some panels was vaunted as rich wood-carving. There was a graceful staircase, and a good wide hall, from which the dining-room and drawing-room opened by opposite doors; behind the last, in the southwest corner of the house, was his study.

There, literally, he lived during the six or seven years in which I knew him after my coming to Cambridge. Summer and winter he sat there among his books, seldom stirring abroad by day except for a walk, and by night yet more rarely. He went to the monthly mid-day dinner of the Saturday Club in Boston; he was very constant at the fortnightly meetings of his whist-club, because he loved the old friends who formed it; he came always to the Dante suppers at Longfellow's, and he was familiarly in and out at Mr. Norton's, of course. But, otherwise, he kept to his study, except for some rare and almost unwilling absences upon university lecturing at Johns Hopkins or at Cornell.

For four years I did not take any summer outing from Cambridge myself, and my associations with Elmwood and with Lowell are more of summer than of winter weather meetings. But often we went our walks through the snows, trudging along between the horsecar tracks which enclosed the only well-broken-out paths in that simple old Cambridge. I date one memorable expression of his from such a walk, when, as we were passing Longfellow's house, in mid-street, he came as near the declaration of his religious faith as he ever did in my presence. He was speaking of the New Testament, and he said, The truth was in it; but they had covered it up with their hagiology. Though he had been bred a Unitarian, and had more and more liberated himself from all creeds, he humorously affected an abiding belief in hell, and similarly contended for the eternal punishment of the wicked. He was of a religious nature, and he was very reverent of other people's religious feelings. He expressed a special tolerance for my own inherited faith, no doubt because Mrs. Lowell was also a Swedenborgian; but I do not think he was interested in it, and I suspect that all religious formulations bored him. In his earlier poems are many intimations and affirmations of belief in an overruling providence, and especially in the God who declares vengeance His and will repay men for their evil deeds, and will right the weak against the strong. I think he never quite lost this, though when, in the last years of his life, I asked him if he believed there was a moral government of the universe, he answered gravely and with a sort of pain, The scale was so vast, and we saw such a little part of it.

As to tine notion of a life after death, I never had any direct or indirect expression from him; but I incline to the opinion that his hold upon this weakened with his years, as it is sadly apt to do with men who have read much and thought much: they have apparently exhausted their potentialities of psychological life. Mystical Lowell was, as every poet must be, but I do not think he liked mystery. One morning he told me that when he came home the night before he had seen the Doppelganger of one of his household: though, as he joked, he was not in a state to see double.

He then said he used often to see people's Doppelganger; at another time, as to ghosts, he said, He was like Coleridge: he had seen too many of 'em. Lest any weaker brethren should be caused to offend by the restricted oath which I have reported him using in a moment of transport it may be best to note here that I never heard him use any other imprecation, and this one seldom.

Any grossness of speech was inconceivable of him; now and then, but only very rarely, the human nature of some story "unmeet for ladies" was too much for his sense of humor, and overcame him with amusement which he was willing to impart, and did impart, but so that mainly the human nature of it reached you. In this he was like the other great Cambridge men, though he was opener than the others to contact with the commoner life. He keenly delighted in every native and novel turn of phrase, and he would not undervalue a vital word or a notion picked up out of the road even if it had some dirt sticking to it.

He kept as close to the common life as a man of his patrician instincts and cloistered habits could. I could go to him with any new find about it and be sure of delighting him; after I began making my involuntary and all but unconscious studies of Yankee character, especially in the country, he was always glad to talk them over with me. Still, when I had discovered a new accent or turn of speech in the fields he had cultivated, I was aware of a subtle grudge mingling with his pleasure; but this was after all less envy than a fine regret.

At the time I speak of there was certainly nothing in Lowell's dress or bearing that would have kept the common life aloof from him, if that life were not always too proud to make advances to any one. In this retrospect, I see him in the sack coat and rough suit which he wore upon all out-door occasions, with heavy shoes, and a round hat. I never saw him with a high hat on till he came home after his diplomatic stay in London; then he had become rather rigorously correct in his costume, and as conventional as he had formerly been indifferent. In both epochs he was apt to be gloved, and the strong, broad hands, which left the sensation of their vigor for some time after they had clasped yours, were notably white. At the earlier period, he still wore his auburn hair somewhat long; it was darker than his beard, which was branching and full, and more straw-colored than auburn, as were his thick eyebrows; neither hair nor beard was then touched with gray, as I now remember. When he uncovered, his straight, wide, white forehead showed itself one of the most beautiful that could be; his eyes were gay with humor, and alert with all intelligence. He had an enchanting smile, a laugh that was full of friendly joyousness, and a voice that was exquisite music. Everything about him expressed his strenuous physical condition: he would not wear an overcoat in the coldest Cambridge weather; at all times he moved vigorously, and walked with a quick step, lifting his feet well from the ground.

VII.

It gives me a pleasure which I am afraid I cannot impart, to linger in this effort to materialize his presence from the fading memories of the past. I am afraid I can as little impart a due sense of what he spiritually was to my knowledge. It avails nothing for me to say that I think no man of my years and desert had ever so true and constant a friend. He was both younger and older than I by insomuch as he was a poet through and through, and had been out of college before I was born. But he had already come to the age of self-distrust when a man likes to take counsel with his juniors as with his elders, and fancies he can correct his perspective by the test of their fresher vision. Besides, Lowell was most simply and pathetically reluctant to part with youth, and was willing to cling to it wherever he found it. He could not in any wise bear to be left-out. When Mr. Bret Harte came to Cambridge, and the talk was all of the brilliant character-poems with which he had then first dazzled the world, Lowell casually said, with a most touching, however ungrounded sense of obsolescence, He could remember when the 'Biglow Papers' were all the talk. I need not declare that there was nothing ungenerous in that. He was only too ready to hand down his laurels to a younger man; but he wished to do it himself. Through the modesty that is always a quality of such a nature, he was magnanimously sensitive to the appearance of fading interest; he could not take it otherwise than as a proof of his fading power. I had a curious hint of this when one year in making up the prospectus of the Magazine for the next, I omitted his name because I had nothing special to promise from him, and because I was half ashamed to be always flourishing it in the eyes of the public. "I see that you have dropped me this year," he wrote, and I could see that it had hurt, and I knew that he was glad to believe the truth when I told him.

He did not care so much for popularity as for the praise of his friends. If he liked you he wished you not only to like what he wrote, but to say so. He was himself most cordial in his recognition of the things that pleased him. What happened to me from him, happened to others, and I am only describing his common habit when I say that nothing I did to his liking failed to bring me a spoken or oftener a written acknowledgment. This continued to the latest years of his life when the effort even to give such pleasure must have cost him a physical pang.

He was of a very catholic taste; and he was apt to be carried away by a little touch of life or humor, and to overvalue the piece in which he found it; but, mainly his judgments of letters and men were just. One of the dangers of scholarship was a peculiar danger in the Cambridge keeping, but Lowell was almost as averse as Longfellow from contempt. He could snub, and pitilessly, where he thought there was presumption and apparently sometimes merely because he was in the mood; but I cannot remember ever to have heard him sneer. He was often wonderfully patient of tiresome people, and sometimes celestially insensible to vulgarity. In spite of his reserve, he really wished people to like him; he was keenly alive to neighborly good-will or ill-will; and when there was a question of widening Elmwood avenue by taking part of his grounds, he was keenly hurt by hearing that some one who lived near him had said he hoped the city would cut down Lowell's elms: his English elms, which his father had planted, and with which he was himself almost one blood!

VIII.

In the period of which I am speaking, Lowell was constantly writing and pretty constantly printing, though still the superstition held that he was an idle man. To this time belongs the publication of some of his finest poems, if not their inception: there were cases in which their inception dated far back, even to ten or twenty years. He wrote his poems at a heat, and the manuscript which came to me for the magazine was usually the first draft, very little corrected. But if the cold fit took him quickly it might hold him so fast that he would leave the poem in abeyance till he could slowly live back to a liking for it.

The most of his best prose belongs to the time between 1866 and 1874, and to this time we owe the several volumes of essays and criticisms called 'Among My Books' and 'My Study Windows'. He wished to name these more soberly, but at the urgence of his publishers he gave them titles which they thought would be attractive to the public, though he felt that they took from the dignity of his work. He was not a good business man in a literary way, he submitted to others' judgment in all such matters. I doubt if he ever put a price upon anything he sold, and I dare say he was usually surprised at the largeness of the price paid him; but sometimes if his need was for a larger sum, he thought it too little, without reference to former payments. This happened with a long poem in the Atlantic, which I had urged the counting-room authorities to deal handsomely with him for. I did not know how many hundred they gave him, and when I met him I ventured to express the hope that the publishers had done their part. He held up four fingers, "Quattro," he said in Italian, and then added with a disappointment which he tried to smile away, "I thought they might have made it cinque."

Between me and me I thought quattro very well, but probably Lowell had in mind some end which cinque would have fitted better. It was pretty sure to be an unselfish end, a pleasure to some one dear to him, a gift that he had wished to make. Long afterwards when I had been the means of getting him cinque for a poem one-tenth the length, he spoke of the payment to me. "It came very handily; I had been wanting to give a watch."

I do not believe at any time Lowell was able to deal with money

"Like wealthy men, not knowing what they give."

more probably he felt a sacredness in the money got by literature, which the literary man never quite rids him self of, even when he is not a poet, and which made him wish to dedicate it to something finer than the every day uses. He lived very quietly, but he had by no means more than he needed to live upon, and at that time he had pecuniary losses. He was writing hard, and was doing full work in his Harvard professorship, and he was so far dependent upon his salary, that he felt its absence for the year he went abroad. I do not know quite how to express my sense of something unworldly, of something almost womanlike in his relation to money.

He was not only generous of money, but he was generous of himself, when he thought he could be of use, or merely of encouragement. He came all the way into Boston to hear certain lectures of mine on the Italian poets, which he could not have found either edifying or amusing, that he might testify his interest in me, and show other people that they were worth coming to. He would go carefully over a poem with me, word by word, and criticise every turn of phrase, and after all be magnanimously tolerant of my sticking to phrasings that he disliked. In a certain line

"The silvern chords of the piano trembled,"

he objected to silvern. Why not silver? I alleged leathern, golden, and like adjectives in defence of my word; but still he found an affectation in it, and suffered it to stand with extreme reluctance. Another line of another piece:

"And what she would, would rather that she would not"

he would by no means suffer. He said that the stress falling on the last word made it "public-school English," and he mocked it with the answer a maid had lately given him when he asked if the master of the house was at home. She said, "No, sir, he is not," when she ought to have said "No, sir, he isn't." He was appeased when I came back the next day with the stanza amended so that the verse could read:

"And what she would, would rather she would not so"

but I fancy he never quite forgave my word silvern. Yet, he professed not to have prejudices in such matters, but to use any word that would serve his turn, without wincing; and he certainly did use and defend words, as undisprivacied and disnatured, that made others wince.

He was otherwise such a stickler for the best diction that he would not have had me use slovenly vernacular even in the dialogue in my stories: my characters must not say they wanted to do so and so, but wished, and the like. In a copy of one of my books which I found him reading, I saw he had corrected my erring Western woulds and shoulds; as he grew old he was less and less able to restrain himself from setting people right to their faces. Once, in the vast area of my ignorance, he specified my small acquaintance with a certain period of English poetry, saying, "You're rather shady, there, old fellow." But he would not have had me too learned, holding that he had himself been hurt for literature by his scholarship.

His patience in analyzing my work with me might have been the easy effort of his habit of teaching; and his willingness to give himself and his own was no doubt more signally attested in his asking a brother man of letters who wished to work up a subject in the college library, to stay a fortnight in his house, and to share his study, his beloved study, with him. This must truly have cost him dear, as any author of fixed habits will understand. Happily the man of letters was a good fellow, and knew how to prize the favor-done him, but if he had been otherwise, it would have been the same to Lowell. He not only endured, but did many things for the weaker brethren, which were amusing enough to one in the secret of his inward revolt. Yet in these things he was considerate also of the editor whom he might have made the sharer of his self-sacrifice, and he seldom offered me manuscripts for others. The only real burden of the kind that he put upon me was the diary of a Virginian who had travelled in New England during the early thirties, and had set down his impressions of men and manners there. It began charmingly, and went on very well under Lowell's discreet pruning, but after a while he seemed to fall in love with the character of the diarist so much that he could not bear to cut anything.

IX.

He had a great tenderness for the broken and ruined South, whose sins he felt that he had had his share in visiting upon her, and he was willing to do what he could to ease her sorrows in the case of any particular Southerner. He could not help looking askance upon the dramatic shows of retribution which some of the Northern politicians were working, but with all his misgivings he continued to act with the Republican party until after the election of Hayes; he was away from the country during the Garfield campaign. He was in fact one of the Massachusetts electors chosen by the Republican majority in 1816, and in that most painful hour when there was question of the policy and justice of counting Hayes in for the presidency, it was suggested by some of Lowell's friends that he should use the original right of the electors under the constitution, and vote for Tilden, whom one vote would have chosen president over Hayes. After he had cast his vote for Hayes, he quietly referred to the matter one day, in the moment of lighting his pipe, with perhaps the faintest trace of indignation in his tone. He said that whatever the first intent of the constitution was, usage had made the presidential electors strictly the instruments of the party which chose them, and that for him to have voted for Tilden when he had been chosen to vote for Hayes would have-been an act of bad faith.

He would have resumed for me all the old kindness of our relations before the recent year of his absence, but this had inevitably worked a little estrangement. He had at least lost the habit of me, and that says much in such matters. He was not so perfectly at rest in the Cambridge environment; in certain indefinable ways it did not so entirely suffice him, though he would have been then and always the last to allow this. I imagine his friends realized more than he, that certain delicate but vital filaments of attachment had frayed and parted in alien air, and left him heart-loose as he had not been before.

I do not know whether it crossed his mind after the election of Hayes that he might be offered some place abroad, but it certainly crossed the minds of some of his friends, and I could not feel that I was acting for myself alone when I used a family connection with the President, very early in his term, to let him know that I believed Lowell would accept a diplomatic mission. I could assure him that I was writing wholly without Lowell's privity or authority, and I got back such a letter as I could wish in its delicate sense of the situation. The President said that he had already thought of offering Lowell something, and he gave me the pleasure, a pleasure beyond any other I could imagine, of asking Lowell whether he would accept the mission to Austria. I lost no time carrying his letter to Elmwood, where I found Lowell over his coffee at dinner. He saw me at the threshold, and called to me through the open door to come in, and I handed him the letter, and sat down at table while he ran it through. When he had read it, he gave a quick "Ah!" and threw it over the length of the table to Mrs. Lowell. She read it in a smiling and loyal reticence, as if she would not say one word of all she might wish to say in urging his acceptance, though I could see that she was intensely eager for it. The whole situation was of a perfect New England character in its tacit significance; after Lowell had taken his coffee we turned into his study without further allusion to the matter.

A day or two later he came to my house to say that he could not accept the Austrian mission, and to ask me to tell the President so for him, and make his acknowledgments, which he would also write himself. He remained talking a little while of other things, and when he rose to go, he said with a sigh of vague reluctance, "I should like to see a play of Calderon," as if it had nothing to do with any wish of his that could still be fulfilled. "Upon this hint I acted," and in due time it was found in Washington, that the gentleman who had been offered the Spanish mission would as lief go to Austria, and Lowell was sent to Madrid.

X.

When we met in London, some years later, he came almost every afternoon to my lodging, and the story of our old-time Cambridge walks began again in London phrases. There were not the vacant lots and outlying fields of his native place, but we made shift with the vast, simple parks, and we walked on the grass as we could not have done in an American park, and were glad to feel the earth under our feet. I said how much it was like those earlier tramps; and that pleased him, for he wished, whenever a thing delighted him, to find a Cambridge quality in it.

But he was in love with everything English, and was determined I should be so too, beginning with the English weather, which in summer cannot be overpraised. He carried, of course, an umbrella, but he would not put it up in the light showers that caught us at times, saying that the English rain never wetted you. The thick short turf delighted him; he would scarcely allow that the trees were the worse for foliage blighted by a vile easterly storm in the spring of that year. The tender air, the delicate veils that the moisture in it cast about all objects at the least remove, the soft colors of the flowers, the dull blue of the low sky showing through the rifts of the dirty white clouds, the hovering pall of London smoke, were all dear to him, and he was anxious that I should not lose anything of their charm.

He was anxious that I should not miss the value of anything in England, and while he volunteered that the aristocracy had the corruptions of aristocracies everywhere, he insisted upon my respectful interest in it because it was so historical. Perhaps there was a touch of irony in this demand, but it is certain that he was very happy in England. He had come of the age when a man likes smooth, warm keeping, in which he need make no struggle for his comfort; disciplined and obsequious service; society, perfectly ascertained within the larger society which we call civilization; and in an alien environment, for which he was in no wise responsible, he could have these without a pang of the self-reproach which at home makes a man unhappy amidst his luxuries, when he considers their cost to others. He had a position which forbade thought of unfairness in the conditions; he must not wake because of the slave, it was his duty to sleep. Besides, at that time Lowell needed all the rest he could get, for he had lately passed through trials such as break the strength of men, and how them with premature age. He was living alone in his little house in Lowndes Square, and Mrs. Lowell was in the country, slowly recovering from the effects of the terrible typhus which she had barely survived in Madrid. He was yet so near the anguish of that experience that he told me he had still in his nerves the expectation of a certain agonized cry from her which used to rend them. But he said he had adjusted himself to this, and he went on to speak with a patience which was more affecting in him than in men of more phlegmatic temperament, of how we were able to adjust ourselves to all our trials and to the constant presence of pain. He said he was never free of a certain distress, which was often a sharp pang, in one of his shoulders, but his physique had established such relations with it that, though he was never unconscious of it, he was able to endure it without a recognition of it as suffering.

He seemed to me, however, very well, and at his age of sixty-three, I could not see that he was less alert and vigorous than he was when I first knew him in Cambridge. He had the same brisk, light step, and though his beard was well whitened and his auburn hair had grown ashen through the red, his face had the freshness and his eyes the clearness of a young man's. I suppose the novelty of his life kept him from thinking about his years; or perhaps in contact with those great, insenescent Englishmen, he could not feel himself old. At any rate he did not once speak of age, as he used to do ten years earlier, and I, then half through my forties, was still "You young dog" to him. It was a bright and cheerful renewal of the early kindliness between us, on which indeed there had never been a shadow, except such as distance throws. He wished apparently to do everything he could to assure us of his personal interest; and we were amused to find him nervously apprehensive of any purpose, such as was far from us, to profit by him officially. He betrayed a distinct relief when he found we were not going to come upon him even for admissions to the houses of parliament, which we were to see by means of an English acquaintance. He had not perhaps found some other fellow-citizens so considerate; he dreaded the half-duties of his place, like presentations to the queen, and complained of the cheap ambitions he had to gratify in that way.

He was so eager to have me like England in every way, and seemed so fond of the English, that I thought it best to ask him whether he minded my quoting, in a paper about Lexington, which I was just then going to print in a London magazine, some humorous lines of his expressing the mounting satisfaction of an imaginary Yankee story-teller who has the old fight terminate in Lord Percy's coming

"To hammer stone for life in Concord jail."

It had occurred to me that it might possibly embarrass him to have this patriotic picture presented to a public which could not take our Fourth of July pleasure in it, and I offered to suppress it, as I did afterwards quite for literary reasons. He said, No, let it stand, and let them make the worst of it; and I fancy that much of his success with a people who are not gingerly with other people's sensibilities came from the frankness with which he trampled on their prejudice when he chose. He said he always told them, when there was question of such things, that the best society he had ever known was in Cambridge, Massachusetts. He contended that the best English was spoken there; and so it was, when he spoke it.

We were in London out of the season, and he was sorry that he could not have me meet some titles who he declared had found pleasure in my books; when we returned from Italy in the following June, he was prompt to do me this honor. I dare say he wished me to feel it to its last implication, and I did my best, but there was nothing in the evening I enjoyed so much as his coming up to Mrs. Lowell, at the close, when there was only a title or two left, and saying to her as he would have said to her at Elmwood, where she would have personally planned it, "Fanny, that was a fine dinner you gave us." Of course, this was in a tender burlesque; but it remains the supreme impression of what seemed to me a cloudlessly happy period for Lowell. His wife was quite recovered of her long suffering, and was again at the head of his house, sharing in his pleasures, and enjoying his successes for his sake; successes so great that people spoke of him seriously, as "an addition to society" in London, where one man more or less seemed like a drop in the sea. She was a woman perfectly of the New England type and tradition: almost repellantly shy at first, and almost glacially cold with new acquaintance, but afterwards very sweet and cordial. She was of a dark beauty with a regular face of the Spanish outline; Lowell was of an ideal manner towards her, and of an admiration which delicately travestied itself and which she knew how to receive with smiling irony. After her death, which occurred while he was still in England, he never spoke of her to me, though before that he used to be always bringing her name in, with a young lover-like fondness.

XI.

In the hurry of the London season I did not see so much of Lowell on our second sojourn as on our first, but once when we were alone in his study there was a return to the terms of the old meetings in Cambridge. He smoked his pipe, and sat by his fire and philosophized; and but for the great London sea swirling outside and bursting through our shelter, and dashing him with notes that must be instantly answered, it was a very fair image of the past. He wanted to tell me about his coachman whom he had got at on his human side with great liking and amusement, and there was a patient gentleness in his manner with the footman who had to keep coming in upon him with those notes which was like the echo of his young faith in the equality of men. But he always distinguished between the simple unconscious equality of the ordinary American and its assumption by a foreigner. He said he did not mind such an American's coming into his house with his hat on; but if a German or Englishman did it, he wanted to knock it off. He was apt to be rather punctilious in his shows of deference towards others, and at one time he practised removing his own hat when he went into shops in Cambridge. It must have mystified the Cambridge salesmen, and I doubt if he kept it up.

With reference to the doctrine of his young poetry, the fierce and the tender humanity of his storm and stress period, I fancy a kind of baffle in Lowell, which I should not perhaps find it easy to prove. I never knew him by word or hint to renounce this doctrine, but he could not come to seventy years without having seen many high hopes fade, and known many inspired prophecies fail. When we have done our best to make the world over, we are apt to be dismayed by finding it in much the old shape. As he said of the moral government of the universe, the scale is so vast, and a little difference, a little change for the better, is scarcely perceptible to the eager consciousness of the wholesale reformer. But with whatever sense of disappointment, of doubt as to his own deeds for truer freedom and for better conditions I believe his sympathy was still with those who had some heart for hoping and striving. I am sure that though he did not agree with me in some of my own later notions for the redemption of the race, he did not like me the less but rather the more because (to my own great surprise I confess) I had now and then the courage of my convictions, both literary and social.

He was probably most at odds with me in regard to my theories of fiction, though he persisted in declaring his pleasure in my own fiction. He was in fact, by nature and tradition, thoroughly romantic, and he could not or would not suffer realism in any but a friend. He steadfastly refused even to read the Russian masters, to his immense loss, as I tried to persuade him, and even among the modern Spaniards, for whom he might have had a sort of personal kindness from his love of Cervantes, he chose one for his praise the least worthy, of it, and bore me down with his heavier metal in argument when I opposed to Alarcon's factitiousness the delightful genuineness of Valdes. Ibsen, with all the Norwegians, he put far from him; he would no more know them than the Russians; the French naturalists he abhorred. I thought him all wrong, but you do not try improving your elders when they have come to three score and ten years, and I would rather have had his affection unbroken by our difference of opinion than a perfect agreement. Where he even imagined that this difference could work me harm, he was anxious to have me know that he meant me none; and he was at the trouble to write me a letter when a Boston paper had perverted its report of what he said in a public lecture to my disadvantage, and to assure me that he had not me in mind. When once he had given his liking, he could not bear that any shadow of change should seem to have come upon him. He had a most beautiful and endearing ideal of friendship; he desired to affirm it and to reaffirm it as often as occasion offered, and if occasion did not offer, he made occasion. It did not matter what you said or did that contraried him; if he thought he had essentially divined you, you were still the same: and on his part he was by no means exacting of equal demonstration, but seemed not even to wish it.

XII.

After he was replaced at London by a minister more immediately representative of the Democratic administration, he came home. He made a brave show of not caring to have remained away, but in truth he had become very fond of England, where he had made so many friends, and where the distinction he had, in that comfortably padded environment, was so agreeable to him.

It would have been like him to have secretly hoped that the new President might keep him in London, but he never betrayed any ignoble disappointment, and he would not join in any blame of him. At our first meeting after he came home he spoke of the movement which had made Mr. Cleveland president, and said he supposed that if he had been here, he should have been in it. All his friends were, he added, a little helplessly; but he seemed not to dislike my saying I knew one of his friends who was not: in fact, as I have told, he never disliked a plump difference—unless he disliked the differer.

For several years he went back to England every summer, and it was not until he took up his abode at Elmwood again that he spent a whole year at home. One winter he passed at his sister's home in Boston, but mostly he lived with his daughter at Southborough. I have heard a story of his going to Elmwood soon after his return in 1885, and sitting down in his old study, where he declared with tears that the place was full of ghosts. But four or five years later it was well for family reasons that he should live there; and about the same time it happened that I had taken a house for the summer in his neighborhood. He came to see me, and to assure me, in all tacit forms of his sympathy in a sorrow for which there could be no help; but it was not possible that the old intimate relations should be resumed. The affection was there, as much on his side as on mine, I believe; but he was now an old man and I was an elderly man, and we could not, without insincerity, approach each other in the things that had drawn us together in earlier and happier years. His course was run; my own, in which he had taken such a generous pleasure, could scarcely move his jaded interest. His life, so far as it remained to him, had renewed itself in other air; the later friendships beyond seas sufficed him, and were without the pang, without the effort that must attend the knitting up of frayed ties here.

He could never have been anything but American, if he had tried, and he certainly never tried; but he certainly did not return to the outward simplicities of his life as I first knew it. There was no more round-hat-and-sack-coat business for him; he wore a frock and a high hat, and whatever else was rather like London than Cambridge; I do not know but drab gaiters sometimes added to the effect of a gentleman of the old school which he now produced upon the witness. Some fastidiousnesses showed themselves in him, which were not so surprising. He complained of the American lower class manner; the conductor and cabman would be kind to you but they would not be respectful, and he could not see the fun of this in the old way. Early in our acquaintance he rather stupified me by saying, "I like you because you don't put your hands on me," and I heard of his consenting to some sort of reception in those last years, "Yes, if they won't shake hands."

Ever since his visit to Rome in 1875 he had let his heavy mustache grow long till it dropped below the corners of his beard, which was now almost white; his face had lost the ruddy hue so characteristic of him. I fancy he was then ailing with premonitions of the disorder which a few years later proved mortal, but he still bore himself with sufficient vigor, and he walked the distance between his house and mine, though once when I missed his visit the family reported that after he came in he sat a long time with scarcely a word, as if too weary to talk. That winter, I went into Boston to live, and I saw him only at infrequent intervals, when I could go out to Elmwood. At such times I found him sitting in the room which was formerly the drawing-room, but which had been joined with his study by taking away the partitions beside the heavy mass of the old colonial chimney. He told me that when he was a newborn babe, the nurse had carried him round this chimney, for luck, and now in front of the same hearth, the white old man stretched himself in an easy-chair, with his writing-pad on his knees and his books on the table at his elbow, and was willing to be entreated not to rise. I remember the sun used to come in at the eastern windows full pour, and bathe the air in its warmth.

He always hailed me gayly, and if I found him with letters newly come from England, as I sometimes did, he glowed and sparkled with fresh life. He wanted to read passages from those letters, he wanted to talk about their writers, and to make me feel their worth and charm as he did. He still dreamed of going back to England the next summer, but that was not to be. One day he received me not less gayly than usual, but with a certain excitement, and began to tell me about an odd experience he had had, not at all painful, but which had very much mystified him. He had since seen the doctor, and the doctor had assured him that there was nothing alarming in what had happened, and in recalling this assurance, he began to look at the humorous aspects of the case, and to make some jokes about it. He wished to talk of it, as men do of their maladies, and very fully, and I gave him such proof of my interest as even inviting him to talk of it would convey. In spite of the doctor's assurance, and his joyful acceptance of it, I doubt if at the bottom of his heart there was not the stir of an uneasy misgiving; but he had not for a long time shown himself so cheerful.

It was the beginning of the end. He recovered and relapsed, and recovered again; but never for long. Late in the spring I came out, and he had me stay to dinner, which was somehow as it used to be at two o'clock; and after dinner we went out on his lawn. He got a long-handled spud, and tried to grub up some dandelions which he found in his turf, but after a moment or two he threw it down, and put his hand upon his back with a groan. I did not see him again till I came out to take leave of him before going away for the summer, and then I found him sitting on the little porch in a western corner of his house, with a volume of Scott closed upon his finger. There were some other people, and our meeting was with the constraint of their presence. It was natural in nothing so much as his saying very significantly to me, as if he knew of my heresies concerning Scott, and would have me know he did not approve of them, that there was nothing he now found so much pleasure in as Scott's novels. Another friend, equally heretical, was by, but neither of us attempted to gainsay him. Lowell talked very little, but he told of having been a walk to Beaver Brook, and of having wished to jump from one stone to another in the stream, and of having had to give it up. He said, without completing the sentence, If it had come to that with him! Then he fell silent again; and with some vain talk of seeing him when I came back in the fall, I went away sick at heart. I was not to see him again, and I shall not look upon his like.

I am aware that I have here shown him from this point and from that in a series of sketches which perhaps collectively impart, but do not assemble his personality in one impression. He did not, indeed, make one impression upon me, but a thousand impressions, which I should seek in vain to embody in a single presentment. What I have cloudily before me is the vision of a very lofty and simple soul, perplexed, and as it were surprised and even dismayed at the complexity of the effects from motives so single in it, but escaping always to a clear expression of what was noblest and loveliest in itself at the supreme moments, in the divine exigencies. I believe neither in heroes nor in saints; but I believe in great and good men, for I have known them, and among such men Lowell was of the richest nature I have known. His nature was not always serene or pellucid; it was sometimes roiled by the currents that counter and cross in all of us; but it was without the least alloy of insincerity, and it was never darkened by the shadow of a selfish fear. His genius was an instrument that responded in affluent harmony to the power that made him a humorist and that made him a poet, and appointed him rarely to be quite either alone.

www.ingramcontent.com/pod-product-compliance
Ingram Content Group UK Ltd.
Pitfield, Milton Keynes, MK11 3LW, UK
UKHW042152281224
453045UK00004B/361